Best Books 9th

E FICTION SCH

9/13

Schwartz, Amy.

Tiny and Hercules

**Please check all items for damages
before leaving the Library.
Thereafter you will be held
responsible for all injuries
to items beyond reasonable wear.**

TINY & Hercules

Amy Schwartz

A NEAL PORTER BOOK
ROARING BROOK PRESS
NEW YORK

For Becky, Debbie, and Joan

A Neal Porter Book

Published by Roaring Brook Press

Roaring Brook Press is a division of Holtzbrinck Publishing Holdings Limited Partnership

175 Fifth Avenue, New York, New York 10010

www.roaringbrookpress.com

Distributed in Canada by H. B. Fenn and Company, Ltd.

Cataloging-in-Publication Data is on file at the Library of Congress.

ISBN-13: 978-1-59643-253-6

ISBN-10: 1-59643-253-5

Roaring Brook Press books are available for special promotions and premiums.

For details contact: Director of Special Markets, Holtzbrinck Publishers.

Printed in China

Book design by Jennifer Browne

First edition May 2009

2 4 6 8 10 9 7 5 3 1

Ice Skating

"Tiny," Hercules said. "There's a letter for you. It has flowers on it."

"Oh no," Tiny said. "It's an invitation to Irma's ice-skating party.
What will I do? I can't ice-skate my way out of a paper bag!"

"Don't worry," Hercules said. "Grab your mittens. I'll teach you."

At the rink, things didn't go quite as planned.

"Oomph, umph, awph," Tiny trumpeted each time he fell.

"Let's stop for hot chocolate," Hercules said. "We'll try again tomorrow."

When the day of the party arrived, Tiny was in a panic.
"Seventeen days of practicing, and I'm worse than when we started."
"Don't worry," Tiny said. "I'll come with you."

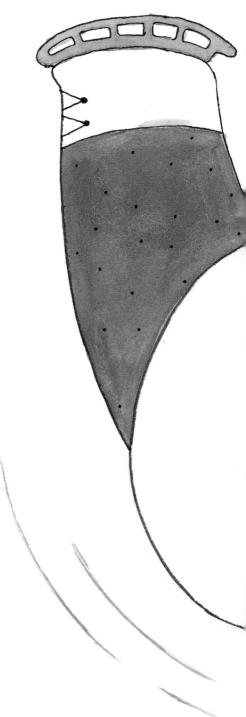

On the ice, things went from bad to worse.

Everyone was snickering into their mittens.

"Don't worry," Hercules said. "I have an idea."

Art

"I need to express myself," Hercules said. "I think I'll take an art class."
"Great idea," Tiny said. "Tomorrow we'll get supplies."

Tiny helped Hercules buy a pad of paper and a paint set.
"Now I'm ready," Hercules said.
He signed up for an art class at the museum.

"Students," the art teacher said. "Art is GRAND.
Art is BIG. Art is STUPENDOUS. Remember
this when you are doing your homework."

At home, Hercules set up some flowers to paint.

"This isn't working," he said.

Hercules set up some fruit.

"This is a disaster," he said.

Hercules set up a violin and some jugs.

"This is a nightmare," he said to Tiny. "I need something GRAND. I need something BIG. I need something STUPENDOUS."

"Well," Tiny said. "I think I can help you out."

Lemonade

"Hercules," Tiny said. "Let's have a lemonade stand."

"Great idea!" Hercules said. "We'll serve cookies, too. Three kinds."

All morning Hercules
squeezed lemons and
measured sugar.

Tiny baked cookies and built a
beautiful lemonade stand. He set out
a table and chairs.

"I'll be the waiter," he told Hercules.

Two boys came by.
"Two lemonades and two oatmeal raisins," they ordered.
"Coming right up," Tiny said.

A little girl and her mother walked up.
"Two lemonades, one chocolate cookie, and one mint," the mother said.
"My pleasure," Tiny replied.

Two fancy ladies sat down.

"May I help you?" Tiny said.

"We'd like two glasses of lemonade, extra sugar, two mint cookies, I mean three chocolate cookies. I mean two oatmeal raisin," the first lady said.

Tiny came back carrying a large tray.

"This isn't what I ordered!" the first lady complained.
"I wanted no sugar and three mint cookies! Manager!"
   "I've never seen such terrible service!" the second lady said.
Tiny looked like he might cry.
Hercules had to do something.

Birthday Party

"Tiny," Hercules said. "Let's have a birthday party for my Uncle Roy. He's 103 tomorrow."

"Great!" Tiny said. "I love parties!"

Hercules baked a cake and spread the frosting. He put on 103 candles.

Tiny delivered the invitations to Hercules' 58 uncles and aunts and cousins.

Hercules decorated the house.

The next day at noon everyone showed up.
The 58 aunts and uncles and cousins played musical chairs,
and pin the tail on the donkey, and had a treasure hunt.

Tiny flashed the lights.

"Cake time!" he called.

The guests gathered round. Hercules lit the candles.

"Make a wish, Uncle Roy."

The guests stepped back.

Uncle Roy screwed up his face. He made a wish.

Then he blew.   And blew.   And blew.

There were 102 candles left.

"Tiny," whispered Hercules. "What should we do?"

"Don't worry," Tiny whispered. "Leave it to me."

Knitting

"Tiny," Hercules said. "Let's do something together."

"Good idea," Tiny said. "How about a class at the Knitting Barn?"

"Excellent," Hercules said.

Tiny and Hercules went shopping for yarn and knitting needles.

"Let's make each other sweaters," Tiny said.

"Uh . . . excellent," Hercules said.

Tiny picked out dotted yellow yarn. Hercules chose bright yellow, blue, and green.

After class, Tiny and Hercules sat by the fire and knit.

"Uh, Tiny . . . I have something to tell you," Hercules said.

"Not now!" Tiny said. "I'm almost done with the armholes."

The next morning, Tiny and Hercules knit in the park.
"Tiny, we should talk," Hercules said.
"Not now!" Tiny said. "I'm just finishing up this sleeve."

In the afternoon, Tiny and Hercules knit over tea.

"Tiny, this can't wait any longer," Hercules said.

"Well neither can this," Tiny said. "I'm done with your sweater! Let's put them on and go for a walk by the lake."

"Tiny, what I've been trying to tell you is that you are a very big elephant. And these are very small knitting needles!"

Tiny looked at the sweater.
"This is the nicest hat I've ever had," he
said. "Now let's go for our walk."

And they did.